Olly
Explores
7 Wonders
OF THE
CHESAPEAKE BAY

Schiffer Publishing Ltd

4880 Lower Valley Road • Atglen, PA 19310

Elaine Ann Allen

ILLUSTRATED BY Kelli Nash

Olly the oyster loved living on the oyster reef with all of his friends. But he missed the days when he traveled in the warm currents of the Chesapeake Bay.

"I want to go exploring," Olly told Mr. Oyster, who was sitting beside him. "I want to go on an adventure."

"How exciting," said Mr. Oyster. "Are you going to see the wonders of the Chesapeake Bay?"

"Wonders?" asked Olly.

"Those are the most wonderful things that we have here on the bay. Just follow the current and you will find them."

So, Olly broke free from his place on the oyster reef and followed the warm current of water. He couldn't wait to find the wonders of the Chesapeake Bay.

"What will they look like?" he wondered. "Where will I find them?"

Olly swam for the shore. Maybe he'd find something there. But when Olly reached the surface, a large beak tried to scoop him up!

"Help!" he cried out.

"Quick, over here!" a snail called from nearby.

Olly hurried behind the tall stems of cord grass. "Thank you, Mr. Snail," he said as he caught his breath. "What is that?"

"That is a Great Blue Heron," said Mr. Snail. "Many of them come to the marsh to look for food."

"It's big," said Olly, feeling very small, "and it has long legs."

"Yes, it's a wading bird," explained Mr. Snail. "Wading birds can walk around in the marsh. They like to eat sea animals, so you had better stay here where you can be safe."

"Oh, but I can't stay," Olly said. "I'm going on an adventure."

"Suit yourself," said Mr. Snail. Olly thought for a moment. It might be best to wait until the Great Blue Heron had gone away. So, Olly decided to stay for just a little while.

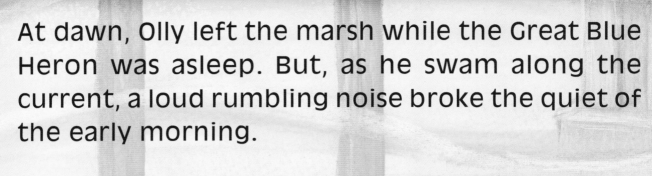

At dawn, Olly left the marsh while the Great Blue Heron was asleep. But, as he swam along the current, a loud rumbling noise broke the quiet of the early morning.

RUMBLE! RUMBLE! RUMBLE!

Olly found a mud flat and burrowed into the mud to cover his ears.

"Is there something wrong, little oyster?!" asked a fiddler crab in a booming voice.

"It's coming from the Chesapeake Bay Bridge!" bellowed Mr. Fiddler Crab. "Cars and trucks use it to pass from one side of the bay to the other. Before the bridge was built, people used boats to cross the bay."

"It sure is big!" shouted Olly.

"You bet! There are actually two bridges, one for cars going east and one for cars going west. Why don't you stay here with me? You can help me look for food in the mud while we watch the cars go by."

"I'm sorry, but I can't!" Olly yelled.

"Maybe next time!" hollered Mr. Fiddler Crab before he plowed through the mud.

Olly thought for a moment. It did look like fun, and the noise wasn't so bad. Maybe he'd stay, for just a little while.

The next morning, Olly swam into the current once again. It was nice to get away from the noise.

"But, I must hurry," he thought to himself, "or I will never find the wonders of the Chesapeake Bay." Olly was in such a hurry that he bumped right into the hull of a sailboat.

"Ouch!" he cried.

"Are you all right?" asked a blue crab who was sitting nearby.

"Yes, ma'am," said Olly, "but that boat was in my way."

"That's a skipjack," said Mrs. Blue Crab. "Skip-jacks are wooden boats that were made many years ago by oystermen right here on the Chesapeake Bay."

"Oystermen?" asked Olly. He didn't like the sound of that word.

"Yes," said the blue crab in a somber tone. "Skipjacks were made to dredge for oysters."

"Oh no!" Olly cried. "I need to get out of here!"

"Don't worry, little oyster. Skipjacks today are mostly used to teach people about the bay. Would you like to stay here with me in the sea grass? You will be safe here."

Olly's head was very sore, and he could use a rest. "Okay, but not for long," he said.

The next morning, Olly continued on his journey. But soon the choppy bay water turned very calm, and he was afraid that he must be lost.

"Excuse me," he asked a rockfish who was swimming nearby, "where are we?"

"We are in the Choptank River," said Mrs. Rockfish.

"River?" said Olly. He wondered how he could have gotten into a river when he had just been in the bay.

"There are many rivers and streams that lead into the bay; they are called tributaries," explained Mrs. Rockfish.

Chesapeake Bay

Baltimore, MD

Washington, DC

Chesapeake
Bay Bridge

Patuxent
River

Choptank River
Bridge & Pier

Calvert Cliffs

Potomac
River

Rappahannock
River

York River

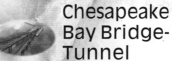

James River

Chesapeake
Bay Bridge-
Tunnel

Cape Henry
Lighthouses

Norfolk, VA

"Oh!" Olly said. "But what are all those people doing?" he wanted to know.

"They are fishing off a pier," said Mrs. Rockfish. "So, we will keep our distance. It is part of the old Choptank River Bridge. It was dedicated by President Franklin D. Roosevelt many years ago."

"I know who that is," declared Olly. "His face is on the dime." Olly liked coins. He had seen them on the sandy bottom of the bay.

"That's right!" said Mrs. Rockfish. "Now there is a new bridge and the old one is used as a pier. Would you like to swim with me? I have come to lay my eggs, and I could use the company."

"I have to go. I'm on a journey," explained Olly.

"Please," said Mrs. Rockfish.

"Well…okay," Olly said. He did not want to make Mrs. Rockfish unhappy.

With the morning light, Olly found his way back into the bay. The river had been nice, but it was time to see the wonders.

Olly swam all day, looking for something wonderful. Before long a tall shadow covered the evening sun.

"Pardon me," he asked a barnacle who was sitting on a rock piling, "but what is blocking the sun?"

"Those are the Calvert Cliffs," said Mr. Barnacle. "They were formed many years ago when the land here was covered by water. People come from all over the world to collect fossils along the cliffs. Fossils are what's left of prehistoric animals that lived a long time ago."

"Cool!" Olly said. "What kinds of animals?" He peered along the rocks to try and find one.

"There are fossils from the bones and teeth of whales, sharks, dolphins, rays, crocodiles, and seabirds. Would you like to stay and join me? We can look for fossils together."

"I must be on my way," Olly said sadly. "You see, I'm exploring."

"That's quite all right," said Mr. Barnacle.

Olly thought for a moment. He had never seen fossils before. Perhaps he'd stay for just a short time.

As the morning sun brightened the sky, Olly continued his journey. "Soon," he thought, "I will find the wonders of the Chesapeake Bay."

But it wasn't long before he heard a loud rumbling noise again. He saw another big bridge like the Chesapeake Bay Bridge; but it wasn't as loud because part of it was underwater!

"Pardon me," he asked a sand crab, "that bridge. Is it broken?"

"No, silly," said Mrs. Sand Crab. "That is the Chesapeake Bay Bridge-Tunnel. It has tunnels that go underwater so that ships can pass into the bay."

"It sure is long!" said Olly looking for the end.

"To be sure," agreed Mrs. Sand Crab. "The Bridge-Tunnel is the largest bridge-tunnel complex in the world. It is really a combination of bridges, tunnels and man-made islands."

"Neat!" Olly said, looking at where the bridge disappeared under the water.

"Would you like to stay and help me? I am making my own tunnel right here on the sandy beach."

"Not for long," said Olly.

"It won't take long," said Mrs. Sand Crab.

It would be fun to build a tunnel in the sand, Olly thought. And it wouldn't hurt if he stayed for just a little while.

At break of day, Olly swam into the current once again. But soon the water got very rough. Olly had swum so far that he had gone right out into the ocean! He swam all day, trying to find his way back into the Chesapeake Bay. Finally, Olly found a sea skate who looked friendly.

"Excuse me, sir," he asked, "I'm trying to find my way back to the bay. Can you help me?"

"Not to worry," said Mr. Sea Skate. "Hop on my back." And the sea skate carried Olly back to the mouth of the bay, where he dropped Olly off. "You're on your own now, little oyster. See over there? Those are the Cape Henry Lighthouses. They were built to guide ships into the Chesapeake Bay."

"Guide ships?" asked Olly.

"Yes, a lighthouse shines a bright light onto the bay at night so that sailors can guide their ships a safe distance from the shore. See the older lighthouse, the one made of bricks? It is the oldest lighthouse on the

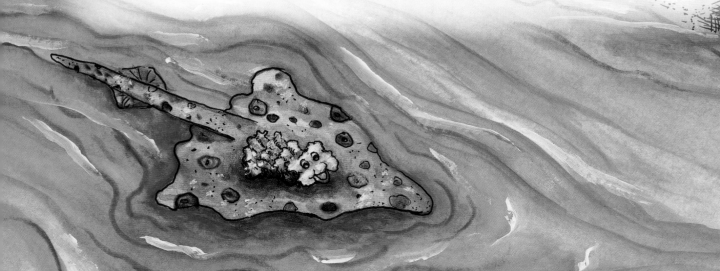

Chesapeake Bay. George Washington himself hired the first lighthouse keeper there."

"He was our first president!" said Olly.

"The new lighthouse replaced the old one when it started to crack. It still shines at night. It will guide you back into the bay."

"Thank you," said Olly, very relieved.

"Don't mention it," said Mr. Sea Skate before he swam on his way.

As the sun set, the glow from the lighthouse guided Olly back into the Chesapeake Bay. Olly was tired. He realized he had been gone for seven days. He had met seven amazing friends, and he had seen seven

wonderful sights. It had been a long journey.

Tomorrow, Olly would go home to the oyster reef, and he would tell Mr. Oyster all about the seven wonders he had explored on the Chesapeake Bay.

Wonderful Facts

1. The Great Blue Heron is the biggest wading bird on the bay. It is over 4 feet tall and its wings stretch to over 6 feet! More than half of all the Great Blue Herons on the Atlantic Coast nest on the bay. They have become a symbol of the Chesapeake Bay.

2. The real name for the Bay Bridge is the William Preston Lane, Jr. Memorial Bay Bridge. More than 27 million cars and trucks pass over it every year! Each side of the bridge is more than 4 miles long and up to 379 feet high. That's taller than the Statue of Liberty!

3. Skipjacks were specially built over 100 years ago to dredge for oysters on the Chesapeake Bay! The skipjack was named after a kind of fish that leaps out of the water, because just like the fish, these boats are nimble and quick. Once there were more than 1,000 skipjacks on the bay; now there are fewer than 20.

4. There are more than 100,000 tributaries in the Chesapeake Bay watershed, the area that drains into the bay. The Choptank River Bridge and Pier is one of the most historic and popular piers in the bay watershed. In 1935, President Franklin D. Roosevelt's yacht *Sequoia* was the first boat to pass through the old drawbridge. The pier is officially named the Bill Burton Fishing Pier.

5. The Calvert Cliffs were formed over 15 million years ago! At that time, part of Maryland was covered by a shallow sea. When the sea eventually pulled away, the Calvert Cliffs were left behind. More than 600 species of fossils have been found along the cliffs!

6. The Chesapeake Bay Bridge-Tunnel is officially named the Lucius J. Kellam, Jr. Bridge-Tunnel. It is more than 20 miles from end to end! When it opened in 1964, it was considered one of seven engineering wonders of the modern world.

7. The Old Cape Henry lighthouse was built in 1792 to make it safe for ships to enter the bay. It was the first lighthouse to be built by our new government after the Revolution. The new lighthouse was built in 1881 when the old one became unsafe. It is the tallest cast iron lighthouse in the United States!